# I Know My Mommy Loves Me

BARBARA WOLFGRAM

*Illustrated by Marlene McAuley*

**CPH**®

**Concordia Publishing House**

This book is dedicated to Joshua.

Dear Parent,

Reading this book with your children will provide you with a wonderful opportunity to relax and enjoy each other. It expresses the delight and security of children in the knowledge of their mother's love. The simple rhyming style and patterned text lend themselves to easy listening and reading. Most of all, the book models language that can be used to articulate to children the love of Jesus.

As you read this book together, take time to listen to your children and share your love with them. Tell them of Jesus' love and help them to know how precious they are in our Lord's eyes. As they feel secure in your love, they will become more and more secure in God's love.

P.S. Be sure to look for the companion book, *I Know My Daddy Loves Me,* also published by Concordia Publishing House.

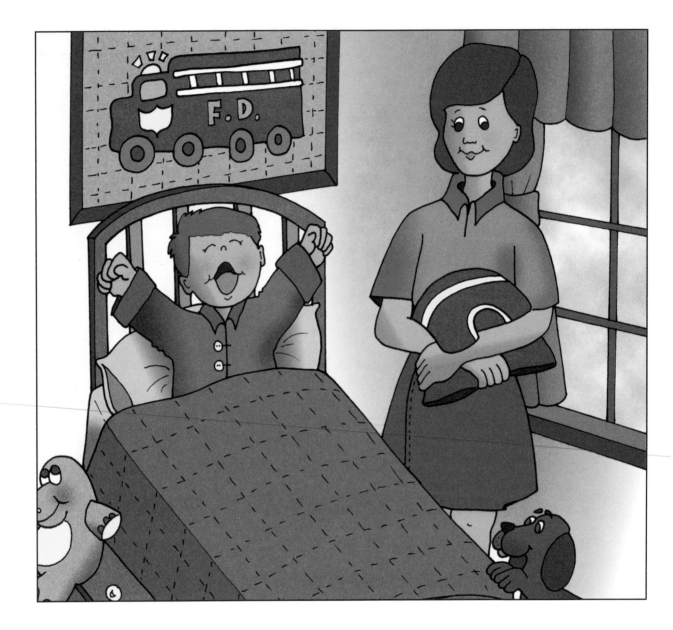

When I wake up my mommy's there
To change my clothes and comb my hair.

I think my mommy loves me.

She calls me *precious, honey, son,*
Her *pumpkin, dear,* and *little one.*

I think my mommy loves me.

My mommy says that Jesus cares
And listens when I say my prayers.

I think my mommy loves me.

She says He watches me each day
And keeps me safe when I'm at play.

I think my mommy loves me.

When she makes treats, I lick the spoon.
And then she helps me clean my room.

I think my mommy loves me.

She lets me win when we race cars.
We fly our spaceship up to Mars.

I think my mommy loves me.

I like it when she reads to me
And helps me learn my ABCs.

I think my mommy loves me.

She teaches me to share my toys
With other little girls and boys.

I think my mommy loves me.

Outside, she lets me pull the weeds.
I help her plant some tiny seeds.

I think my mommy loves me.

We play fun games like hide-and-seek.
I close my eyes, but sometimes peek.

I think my mommy loves me.

We go to places like the zoo,
The cookie store, and mailbox too.

I think my mommy loves me.

She makes up songs and sings to me
And says I'm special as can be.

I think my mommy loves me.

And when it's time for bed at night,
She kisses me and holds me tight.

I think my mommy loves me.

We fold our hands and kneel to pray
And thank God for each special day.

I KNOW my mommy loves me.